SUPERBUNS!

SUPERBUNS!

Kindness Is Her Superpower

DIANE KREDENSOR

SCHOLASTIC INC.

ISBN 978-1-338-67254-1

12 11 10 9 8 7 6 5 4 3 2 1   20 21 22 23 24 25

Printed in the U.S.A.   40

First Scholastic printing, September 2020

Book designed by Laura Lyn DiSiena and Heather Palisi
The illustrations for this book were rendered digitally.
The text of this book was set in Mr. Stickman and Drawzing.

For Charlie Kilgras, kind *and* super

Superbuns was super kind.

listening ears

big caring
eyes

warm
happy smile

fluffy tail
(It's just cute!)

huge
heart

She loved being kind, no matter what her big sister, Blossom, said.

Blossom was 100 percent positive superheroes have powers like . . .

And as Blossom always told Buns:

Kind is kind,

Blossom was a know-it-all.
She knew *everything* about everything.

The bunnies were on their way to Grammy's with a fresh-baked, piping-hot carrot cobbler.

Blossom thought all this kindness was slowing them down.

But Buns couldn't help being super.

Even to her sister.

And after you, too, Miss Fox. I noticed that you've been following us all day.

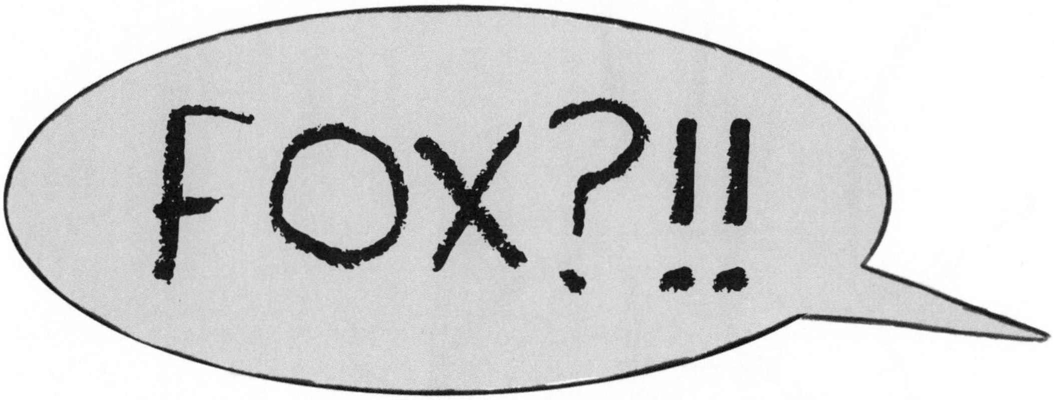
FOX?!!

Blossom knew **exactly** what to do.

Blossom was speechless . . . almost.

LOST?

I know EVERYTHING about being lost. Did you know that the most common lost items are keys, phones, eyeglasses, and shoes? Once, Buns lost her homework, and I found it in Miss Lin's flowerpot. The lost city of Atlantis has never been found. And Roanoke was the Lost Colony. I know that the letters in "lost" can also spell "lots" and "slot" and that "lost" is the past tense form of "lose." And Grammy once told me that I am never lost for words.

And just like that, Blossom learned she didn't know *everything* about everything.

Maybe Buns was right. . . .

Maybe being kind was kind of . . . super.